Olive the Sheep Can't Sleep

Clementina Almeida

Illustrated by
Ana Camila Silva

Charlesbridge

2018 First US edition
Translation copyright © 2018 by Lyn Miller-Lachmann
All rights reserved, including the right of reproduction in whole
or in part in any form. Charlesbridge and colophon are registered
trademarks of Charlesbridge Publishing, Inc.

Published by Charlesbridge
85 Main Street, Watertown, MA 02472
(617) 926-0329 • www.charlesbridge.com

First published in Portugal in 2016 by Porto Editora, S.A.,
Rua da Restauração 365, Porto, Portugal,
as *Olivia a ovelha que não queria dormir*
by Clementina Almeida and Ana Camila Silva
Copyright © Porto Editora and Clementina Almeida 2016

Library of Congress Cataloging-in-Publication Data
Names: Almeida, Clementina, author. | Silva, Ana Camila, illustrator. |
Miller-Lachmann, Lyn, 1956– translator.
Title: Olive the sheep can't sleep / Clementina Almeida;
illustrated by Ana Camila Silva; [translation by Lyn Miller-Lachmann].
Other titles: Olivia, a ovelha que nao queria dormir.
English | Olive the sheep can not sleep
Description: First US edition. | Watertown, MA : Charlesbridge, 2018.
Identifiers: LCCN 2017037945 (print) | LCCN 2017050152 (ebook) |
ISBN 9781632897299 (ebook) | ISBN 9781632897305 (ebook pdf) |
ISBN 9781580898386 (reinforced for library use)
Subjects: LCSH: Bedtime—Juvenile literature. | Child rearing—Juvenile literature.
Classification: LCC HQ784.B43 (ebook) | LCC HQ784.B43 A4613 2018 (print) |
DDC 649/.6—dc23
LC record available at https://lccn.loc.gov/2017037945

Printed in China
(hc) 10 9 8 7 6 5 4 3 2 1

Display type set in Canvas Text Sans by Yellow Design Studio
Text type set in Humper by Typotheticals
Printed by 1010 Printing International Limited in Huizhou, Guangdong, China
Production supervision by Brian G. Walker
Designed by Sarah Richards Taylor

A Note for Grown-Ups

Getting children to go to sleep and
stay asleep is a challenge for most parents
and caregivers, but good sleep habits are
important for the whole family's health.

Throughout this book you'll find helpful hints to
create an effective sleep routine. These simple tips
are based in neuroscience and work for all ages.
They may improve your sleep as well!

Olive was covered in fluffy white fleece. She looked like a cloud on top of four skinny legs.

Olive loved to run through the meadow near the barn, nibbling fresh grass and playing with her friends.

Sneakers

Olive had many friends. She liked to hide from Sneakers the cat, race with Flip the butterfly, and play tricks on Mimi the cow.

Mimi

She played hide-and-seek with Jack the bunny, and she strolled along the creek's edge with Boo the dog.

That is how Olive spent her days, playing
all day long until she tired herself out. YAWN!
But when the sun sank in the sky, sleep was
the furthest thing from Olive's mind.

So Olive's mother made Olive a warm, soothing bath. The smell of lavender rose from the tub.

Mama said, "Watch the soap bubbles, Olive. Fill your chest with air, and then blow the bubbles so they float around you."

"Oh," said Olive, "how lovely!"

1,2,3... 1,2,3,4...

Have the child count to three while breathing in, hold their breath for four counts, and exhale for five counts. Repeat this a few times.

Mama wrapped Olive in a warm, soft towel and sat her on her lap. When she hugged Olive tight, it felt like a big squeeze from head to toe.

It was so nice to sit on Mama's lap, rocking back and forth and listening to her sing.

Place the child on your lap and gently but firmly squeeze their legs, arms, and torso. Slowly rock the child on your lap and sing or hum a soft melody.

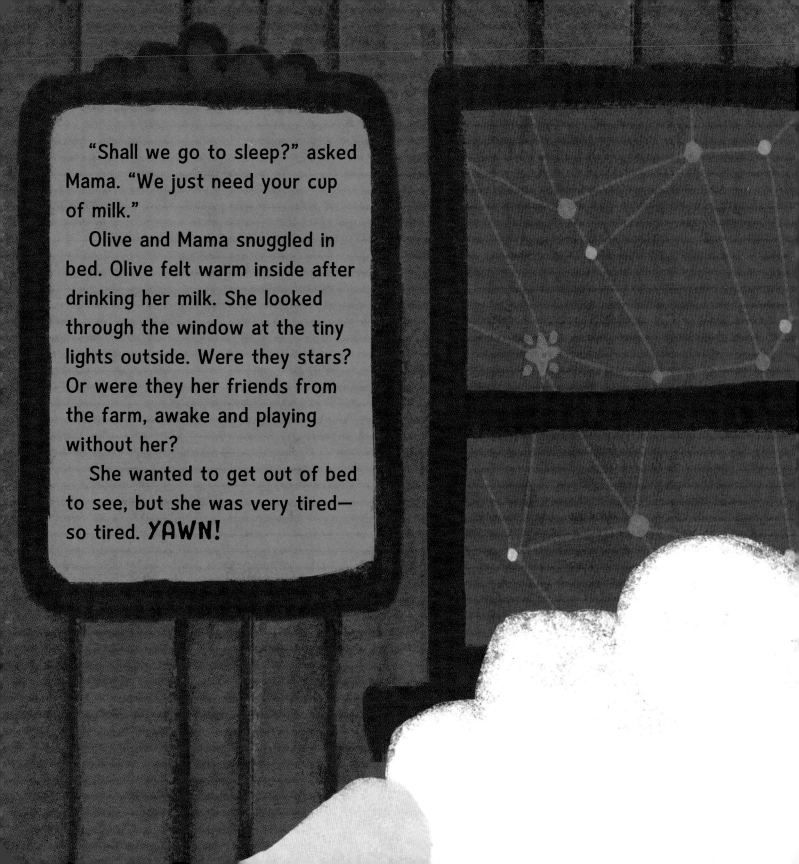

"Shall we go to sleep?" asked Mama. "We just need your cup of milk."

Olive and Mama snuggled in bed. Olive felt warm inside after drinking her milk. She looked through the window at the tiny lights outside. Were they stars? Or were they her friends from the farm, awake and playing without her?

She wanted to get out of bed to see, but she was very tired— so tired. **YAWN!**

Olive curled up, laid her head on the pillow, pulled the covers up to her neck, and decided to *imagine* playing with her friends instead.

"Let's close our eyes," said Mama.

Suggest that the child close their eyes, and very lightly touch their eyelids.

Olive wanted to play with Boo first, but when she pictured him, the dog's eyes were closed.

Olive imagined calling, "Boo! Boo!" but he was in dreamland. She imagined Boo gently curled up inside a feather that slowly, slowly, drifted to the ground.

Boo began to smile, and Olive thought,
"Now he's going to play with me." But Boo
was only dreaming. Snug in his dog bed,
he continued to sleep.

Cuddle with the
child and encourage
soothing imagery.

Olive imagined tiptoeing very slowly to Sneakers's basket, hoping she'd have better luck there. Sneakers's paws were wrapped around his body as if he were giving himself a hug.

Olive imagined quietly calling his name and stroking his fur, but he didn't stir.

Then Sneakers stretched his back legs
gently. It seemed he was almost touching
the stars. Next he stretched his front legs
far, far in front of him.

Olive wanted to do the same.
She stretched her legs out as far as
she could, and slowly relaxed them.
She did it again and again.

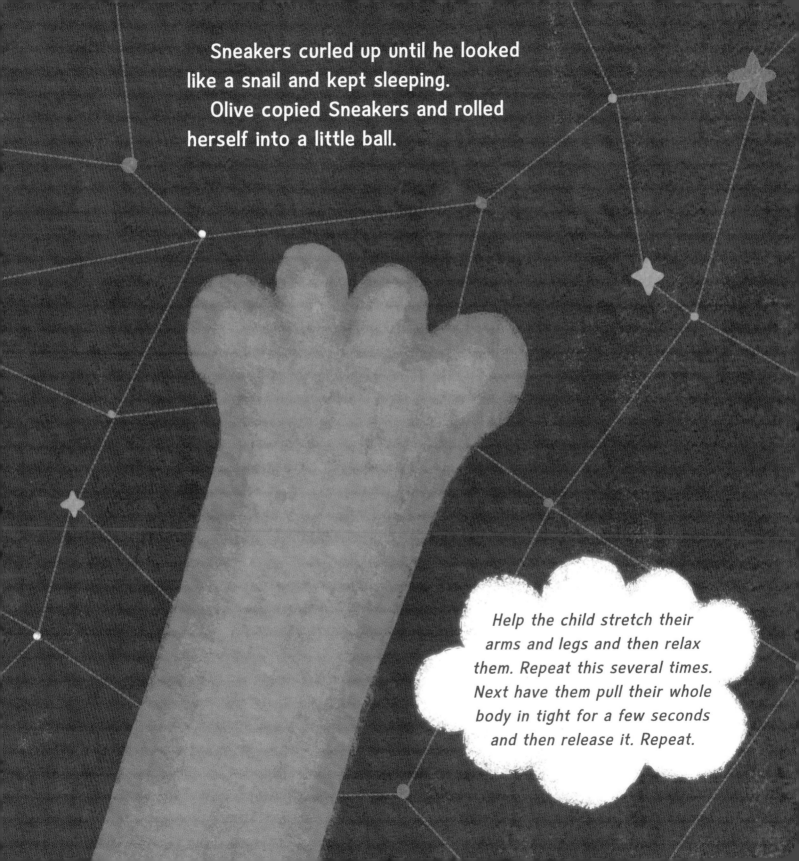

Sneakers curled up until he looked
like a snail and kept sleeping.
Olive copied Sneakers and rolled
herself into a little ball.

*Help the child stretch their
arms and legs and then relax
them. Repeat this several times.
Next have them pull their whole
body in tight for a few seconds
and then release it. Repeat.*

In her imagination, Olive continued walking slowly. She saw Mimi lying down, very relaxed.

From time to time Mimi shrugged her shoulders, and it looked as if she had no neck. Then she lowered her shoulders so her head stuck out like a turtle's. Olive did the same.

Suggest that the child pull their shoulders up tight, release them, and press them down.

Olive's body felt heavy, and her little legs no longer wanted to move.

Olive thought, "I am so sleepy. . . . I want to snuggle in a warm place, like Mimi." YAWN! She imagined a soft, warm breeze rocking her back and forth. She imagined lying down and falling asleep.

Slowly, very slowly, Olive turned over and realized that she was still in her own bed, snuggled under the covers.

Olive was ready to sleep at last. Mama turned out the light and stayed for a few minutes to listen to Olive's soft breathing.

"Sweet dreams, Olive," she whispered.

Keep the child's room quiet, comfortable, and dark.

Bedtime Tips

When children don't get enough sleep, they have more trouble controlling their emotions. They can become irritable and hyperactive, leading to behavioral problems and learning issues. Not sleeping enough hours each day may cause developmental delays as well.

Consistent routines and bedtime rituals are key because they help children prepare for sleep, avoid stress at bedtime, and as a result, go to sleep quickly, waking up rested and relaxed for the new day.

All children are different, and not all tips or solutions will work for everyone. The important thing is to establish a routine adapted to the rhythms of the child and the family's dynamics—and to maintain it as faithfully as possible.

Sleep should be approached as a family priority, not just the child's problem. The routine you choose to establish with your children will work better if they see that the rest of the family also has a bedtime routine, even if it's different from theirs.

Create a routine along with the child.

If the child is old enough, let them take part in making a plan. Never underestimate a child's ability to contribute solutions once they understand the problem. Bedtime represents a moment of separation, and involving children in planning for it gives them a sense of control and security that will help them relax and fall asleep more easily. Bedtime will become a more meaningful and successful family experience when you all plan together.

Choose a transitional object.

To help your child deal with the separation of bedtime, you can leave a little reminder of yourself for comfort and reassurance. A stuffed animal, a doll, or a blanket can offer the child a sense of security and facilitate the process of falling asleep. For maximum effectiveness, include the toy or object throughout the bedtime routine: in the bathtub, putting on pajamas, reading a story, and so on.

Establish a consistent bedtime.

It is important for a child's brain development not only that they sleep enough hours each night but also that they have a consistent bedtime. Establishing a regular time to sleep and a consistent duration helps to improve the quality of sleep. It's best not to vary bedtime (or wake-up time) more than one hour between weeknights and weekends or vacations.

Follow a regular bedtime routine.

A regular bedtime routine helps the child gradually disconnect from daily stimuli, relax, and get ready to sleep. One hour before bedtime, try to avoid all strenuous physical activities and stimulation, such as watching TV or playing games on a tablet or computer. A typical routine includes brushing teeth, putting on pajamas, having a glass of water or a small snack, and a quiet activity (reading a book, listening to calming music, or talking about what happened that day). It's best for the routine to be relatively short—less than forty minutes is fine. A routine of quiet activities helps the child prepare for sleep, and it can also serve as a special time of connection between adult and child.

Make sure the bedroom is comfortable.

The room should be quiet, comfortable, and dark. Some children like to have a nightlight—orange or red light is the most calming. It's important that the child sees the bedroom as a pleasant place, so avoid using it as a location for punishment.

Avoid electronics and bright lights before bed.

TV, computers, tablets, cell phones, and other electronics are not good for sleep, so keep them out of the bedroom. Dimming the lights before going to bed helps prepare the brain for sleep. Light reduces levels of melatonin and stimulates the brain, making us feel wide awake.

Consider having a snack before bed.

It's hard to sleep on an empty stomach. Because children are developing quickly, they may need an extra snack before bed to nourish their bodies. Avoid heavy meals for at least two hours before bedtime, however, and avoid drinks with sugar or caffeine. Healthy options include whole-wheat cereal with milk, crackers or toast, or a piece of fruit.

Get enough exercise, outdoors especially.

Daily exercise is an important part of a healthy lifestyle, and it can also promote a good night's sleep. Time outdoors has a positive effect on sleep as well.

Speak to a specialist.

Some children suffer from specific sleep problems such as insomnia, difficulty getting to sleep, waking in the middle of the night, nightmares, or sleep apnea. It's important to have a specialist evaluate and treat these issues.